TRANSFORMERS™— Robots in Disguise!

They came from Cybertron—a planet of machines—where war raged for thousands of years between the noble Autobots and the evil Decepticons.

NOW THE BATTLE OF THESE POWERFUL ROBOTS IS YOUR BATTLE!

ONLY YOU can protect the earth from the evil destruction of the Decepticons!

Read the directions at the bottom of each page. Then decide what the Autobots should do next.

If you decide correctly, the Autobots will triumph! If you make the wrong choices, the unspeakable evil of the Decepticons will rule the world!

Hurry! The adventure begins on page 1.

Find Your Fate™ Junior Transformers™ #9

THE TRANSFORMERS™

The Invisibility Factor

by Josepha Sherman

BALLANTINE BOOKS • NEW YORK

Library of Congress Catalog Card Number: 86-90733

ISBN: 0-345-33391-8

Editorial Services by Parachute Press, Inc.

Illustrated by William Schmidt

Designed by Gene Siegel

Manufactured in the United States of America

First Edition: September 1986

10 9 8 7 6 5 4 3 2 1

THE TRANSFORMERS™

The Invisibility Factor

It's a cool, clear night in the desert. The sky is crowded with stars, and the only sound is the faint whisper of a breeze. There's no sign of trouble as the Autobots Kup and Hot Rod drive along.

"Earth can be so very beautiful at times like this," observes the old warrior, Kup.

"It sure can," agrees his young friend, Hot Rod. "Even if it doesn't look at all like Cybertron."

"You know, this desert reminds me of something," recalls Kup, who is fond of telling stories of his younger days and the fierce battles he's fought.

"*Everything* reminds you of something else," laughs Hot Rod good-naturedly.

"No, no, really! This is like the desert world of Sonacron V. The Sonites were tiny little insect folks with legs that could—"

"Hey!" Hot Rod interrupts him. "Look at that, up in the sky!"

Kup looks up. "It's just a shooting star. . . . No, it's not. I don't know what it is, but it's coming right toward us!"

. . . .
Turn to page 2.

"Whatever it is, it's blinking on and off!" yells Hot Rod. "Let's see if we can get right under it and check it out."

In minutes, the strange object is low enough in the sky for the Autobots to see it clearly. It certainly isn't a star. It's some type of spacecraft.

Kup and Hot Rod watch as it comes down for a sputtering landing on the other side of a large rock. They hear the clanking, wheezing sounds of damaged engines breaking down.

"I've never seen anything like it," Kup admits, staring at the rickety ship that is patched together from odd parts and scrap metal. One minute the ship is visible, and the next minute it disappears—only to appear again minutes later.

"Let's see who's inside," suggests the impulsive Hot Rod.

Turn to page 69.

2

"Ms. Sanders," says Prowl, "you must give us the secret of your Invisibility Device."

"No!" the young woman says firmly.

"You don't understand," Springer tells her. "We've got to have something that can stop the Decepticons before it's too late!"

"I won't do it!" cries Sarah. "I won't make a—a weapon of war!"

"But—but we're not going to use it on any humans!" Hot Rod tries to tell her. "We only want it to defend ourselves and your planet from the Decepticons!"

"I don't believe you! I don't!" Sarah says. "And I'm getting out of here!"

Turn to page 70.

3

The Autobots silently trail Scavenger and his captive all the way to Decepticon headquarters. The huge mass of buildings looks like some big, ugly monster looming over the Constructicon as he transforms into his robot mode. Before his young woman prisoner can try to run off, she's forced into the main building.

"We've got to follow," whispers Springer.

The Autobots transform into their robot modes and sneak into Decepticon headquarters. They quietly follow Scavenger and his captive through a maze of long, dark corridors. There's the faint hum of machinery all around them, and the dusty smell of old engine oil, but there's nothing to see but blank gray walls.

"Instead of weapons, the Decepticons should build themselves an interior decorator!" whispers Hot Rod with a soft laugh. "This place is *ugly!*"

"Shh!" warns Kup.

Now Scavenger and his captive have reached the end of a wide hallway. And none other than the Decepticon leader, the evil Galvatron, is waiting at the end of it! Quickly the Autobots duck behind some fuel tanks and listen as Galvatron talks to the young woman.

· ·
Turn to page 12.

If you want the Autobots to stand and fight, you must have sand in *your* sensors! The Autobots are completely outnumbered! And soon they're nothing but a pile of spare parts.

It's too bad that they never got to the spacecraft, because it was a messenger craft from the planet Quintesson. These alien allies of the Decepticons were sending news that they would aid the Decepticons in a full-scale attack on Earth. If the Autobots had intercepted the message, maybe they could have stopped the invasion. But since they didn't, the Decepticons and Quintessons soon turn Earth into one big fueling station in the sky.

THE END

"All right, here we go!" Hot Rod tells himself.

Quickly he revs up his turbo-charged engine, wheels about, and, tires squealing, races full speed ahead—right at the oncoming Decepticons! Desperately they shoot at him, but he's coming at them too fast for them to be able to aim!

"But are they going to move?" wonders Hot Rod. "Or am I going to wind up in the biggest auto pileup since . . ."

The Decepticons realize this Autobot is acting insane! He's not going to stop or even slow down! At the last possible moment they all scramble out of his way, crashing into each other, and Hot Rod, lights blazing, zooms right past them! By the time they get themselves straightened out, Hot Rod is long gone and laughing!

"Now to find out where the other Autobots are!" he says to himself as he drives off to find his friends.

You and he will find out on page 9.

Hot Rod and Kup decide to strike while they have the chance. Hot Rod jumps out from behind the rock and fires at Thrust with his laser blaster. Kup is right behind Hot Rod. He manages to wound Galvatron. But no matter how valiantly Kup and Hot Rod fight, they are only two Autobots against a whole squadron of Decepticons. They don't stand a chance.

The Decepticons swarm around them. There is a whizzing sound and the sickening crunch of metal. What happens to Hot Rod and Kup is too sad to think about, so quietly close the book.

THE END

"Here comes Hot Rod!" cries Jazz.

"Looks like you did okay without me," says Hot Rod, glancing around. Suddenly he spots Sarah running toward her spaceship. "Wait!" he cries. "Where are you going?"

"Sorry!" she calls back as she climbs into her spaceship. "What I've just seen has made up my mind. The Invisibility Device is just too dangerous!"

With that, she starts up the ship's engines. They sputter and cough, but she manages to give them enough power to blast off before the Autobots can stop her. The Autobots watch her fly off into the distance.

"Well," says Ultra Magnus, "there goes a brave scientist. In a way she's right. It is too dangerous a weapon to risk having it fall into the wrong hands."

"Thanks to us the device didn't fall into the worst hands of all—the hands of the Decepticons!" says Hot Rod.

"Very true," agrees Kup. "Now let's head for home and I'll tell you the story of the time I saw a similar device on the outer planet of Serton. It was a warm evening, very much like this one, and . . ."

THE END

The Autobots look out at the dark side of the moon. Because there's no sunlight shining on it, it's even blacker than the space around it.

"Can't see a thing on the surface," says Springer. "And we're not picking up anything on the ship's sensors, either. Maybe they're down there, maybe not."

"Suppose we try firing a few blasts," Hot Rod says uncertainly. "Wouldn't they try to shoot back? Then we'd know where they are."

"Too risky," Jazz cuts in. "Then they'd know where *we* are! But I think I have a better plan."

Ultra Magnus considers. What do you think he should do?

. . . .

Do you want him to go with Hot Rod's idea, risky though it may be? Turn to page 40.

Or would you rather have Ultra Magnus listen to what Jazz has in mind? Turn to page 46.

After some careful steering by Springer, the Autobots make it safely back to Earth. But they've lost all trace of the Decepticons.

"The Decepticons could never have survived those asteroids," the Autobots tell each other.

But a few days later—*bam!* An explosion rocks the Autobot city! The Autobots pick themselves up again just in time to hear something screaming down out of the air. It sounds like a missile, but they don't see anything. And then—*wham!* A second explosion shakes Metroplex.

"We're being bombed!" cries Jazz. "But I don't see anyone up there!"

"It's the Decepticons!" says Ultra Magnus grimly. "We shouldn't have given up so easily! Battle stations, everyone! The Decepticons are using the Invisibility Device!"

But you can't fight what you can't see. The Autobots shoot wildly. They don't hit a thing. The invisible missiles continue to rain down on them. And soon all of Metroplex is nothing but a great junkyard.

THE END

"Your name!" Galvatron commands.

The young woman stiffens. "I'm Sarah Sanders. And that's all I'm going to tell you!"

"My spy, Ravage, saw your craft come down in the desert," Galvatron's cruel voice booms. "He tells me that at times the spacecraft became invisible! We have the craft—and you're going to tell us how it works!"

"I'm not going to tell you a thing!" Sarah says defiantly.

"We don't need your help!" thunders Galvatron. "Bombshell is a master at taking over the mind of his victim. Once he injects you with one of his cerebro shells, you will be totally under his control!"

The Insecticon Bombshell steps out of the shadows and looks at Sarah. "I want your mind!" he mutters greedily.

"We can't let them get away with that!" whispers Hot Rod. "We've got to do something!"

But what should the Autobots do? Make a quick decision!

. . . .

Should they barge in and try to save Sarah through a direct attack? Turn to page 36.

Should they try to come up with a trick instead? Turn to page 62.

"If I wipe out Galvatron, maybe I could stop the Decepticons once and for all!" thinks Hot Rod. "It's worth a try!"

But even as Hot Rod begins his charge forward, the screech of jets pierces the air. It's Starscream! He looks down and gives an evil laugh.

"A fool of an Autobot!"

In another second, Hot Rod will be close enough to strike down Galvatron! But Starscream strikes first. Poor Hot Rod! He's an easy target . . . and you could say he gets fired.

THE END

It's a Decepticon! It's the Constructicon Scavenger, rolling quickly across the desert in his steam shovel form.

"He's got something caught in the jaws of his shovel," whispers Springer, "but I can't quite see what—"

Just then a woman's screams hit the Autobots' audio sensors.

"He's got an Earth woman trapped in there!" cries Hot Rod.

It's up to you to decide what to do!

. . . .

If you think the Autobots should attack Scavenger and free the woman right away, turn to page 21.

If you think they'd better follow Scavenger and try to discover where he's taking the woman before trying a rescue, turn to page 4.

14

Prowl's idea works! The drones' infrared scanners pick up the correct emblem, and they let the Autobots pass!

The Autobots hurry into the ship, and Sarah quickly switches the Invisibility Device to "on." The ship flickers on and off for a few minutes, then stays invisible. "The device may only keep us invisible for a few minutes," warns Sarah. "It's not really perfected."

"That's enough time for us to fix the engine," Prowl assures her. "I hope," he adds to himself.

Prowl and Kup set busily to work on the ship's circuitry. "Better hurry!" urges Hot Rod, looking out the window. "Decepticons just came into the courtyard. They don't know where we are yet."

"They will soon," Sarah says grimly. "The device's gauge is turning back to visible, and I can't stop it! There it goes!" she shouts.

"They've spotted us!" yells Hot Rod.

Turn to page 38.

The Autobots head right into the mass of floating asteroids. Some of those rocks are as big as their ship! Suddenly the Autobot ship is in danger of being smashed to bits!

"We can't get through all this!" cries Jazz.

"The Decepticons did it," answers Springer.

"We don't know that for sure!" argues Hot Rod.

"It can't be done!" Jazz says, feeling the ship shake as a small asteroid hits it. "Hurry, Springer, get us out of here!"

. . . .

Do you want the Autobots to listen to Jazz and hurry out of the asteroid belt? Turn to page 11.

Or do you want them to continue on and try to maneuver their way through the asteroids? Turn to page 27.

17

Kup and Hot Rod think it's important to get that Invisibility Device out of Decepticon hands as quickly as possible. They watch as the Decepticon Shockwave rolls the Invisibility Device in the palm of his huge robotic hand. Then he and the other Decepticons move away from the Autobots and head across the desert back toward Decepticon headquarters.

Giving them a small head start, Kup and Hot Rod tell Sarah to wait for them. The Autobots transform into their auto modes to follow the Decepticons. They trail their enemies until the Decepticons descend into a canyon.

Hot Rod is about to follow them down into the canyon, but Kup stops him. "Wait," Kup says. "This reminds me of the old days on Renerian, the time the two of us stopped a Renerian attack by ourselves. All we did was, we—"

"Kup, please!" groans Hot Rod impatiently. "I don't want to be rude, and I'd love to hear it some other time, but we've got to stop the Decepticons, and memories aren't going to help."

"Not so fast, young fellow," laughs Kup. "We can do right here what I once did on Renerian. Listen and learn."

· ·

Turn to page 28 to learn Kup's plan.

Sarah sighs. "This is my Invisibility Device," she says. "Or it will be, if I can ever get it to work properly. I was testing it out here in the desert when my ship broke down."

An Invisibility Device! Kup and Hot Rod stare at each other. Such a device could be a valuable tool for the Autobots in their fight against the Decepticons! What should they do now?

. . . .

Should they just take the Invisibility Device from Sarah, since, after all, it's ultimately for the good of Earth? Turn to page 45.

Or should they try to convince Sarah to use the device to help the Autobots? Turn to page 25.

19

Sand and gravel fly in all directions as the two Autobots race out of the desert. They zoom all the way back to the Autobot city, Metroplex. Soon they're reporting to their leader, Ultra Magnus.

"We must investigate further!" Ultra Magnus agrees.

Quickly he dispatches an Autobot team to return with Kup and Hot Rod. But when the Autobots get back to where they saw the ship land, Springer shakes his head.

"Nothing here but rocks and sand, empty desert as far as I can see."

"But—but there *was* a ship here!" protests Hot Rod. "We saw it!"

"You must have sand in your sensors, Hot Rod," jokes Jazz.

"I'm telling you, there really was a spacecraft here!" cries the bewildered Hot Rod.

What do you think? Is Hot Rod right? Or are the two Autobots having some sort of mechanical breakdown?

. . . .

If you want the Autobots to return to Metroplex and have Hot Rod and Kup checked out for loose wiring, turn to page 68.

If you want them to search the desert for the spacecraft, turn to page 31.

Springer quickly transforms to his robot mode. With a wild shout, he uses his power thrusters and leaps out in front of Scavenger. The startled Constructicon drops the young woman and hastily transforms, preparing to fight. But then the other Autobots show themselves.

"Help!" yells Scavenger, and turns to flee.

Make a quick decision!

If you want the Autobots to pursue Scavenger, turn to page 33.

If you think it's more important to let him escape while you find out what's going on from the young woman, turn to page 65.

"There are too many Decepticons for a direct attack," muses Prowl. "But what if . . . ? . . . *Yes!*"

Quickly he whispers his plan to the others. Hot Rod nods and races out into the open.

"Hey, you junkyard relics!" he yells at the Decepticons. "Here I am! Come and get me!"

The Decepticons are still angry at having lost the Autobots the first time. In fact, they're too angry to think clearly. Before the furious Decepticon leader, Galvatron, can stop them, they roar off after Hot Rod, leaving only Galvatron, Scavenger, and Shockwave behind.

"Wait!" shouts Galvatron. "Come back, you fools! It's a—"

Just then the Autobots come zooming down at him.

"—trap," finishes Galvatron angrily.

It's more than just a trap. Soon Scavenger is scavenged, Shockwave is shocked, and Galvatron hastily takes to the air, leaving Sarah's spacecraft behind. The sound of his voice drifts back down to the Autobots.

"I'll . . . get . . . you . . . for . . . this, . . . Autobots!"

Springer laughs. "I won't hold my breath! Hey, but what's happened to Hot Rod?"

To find out, turn to page 37.

With the young woman safe in their midst, the Autobots run down the hall.

"W-wait!" Sarah pants. "You—you're so big! I—I can't keep up with you!"

"With your permission, Ms. Sanders," says Prowl politely, and scoops her up.

"Never mind the formalities!" yells Hot Rod. "Here come the Decepticons!"

The Autobots race on at top speed, firing at Decepticons as they go. "Quick!" shouts Sarah. "I heard them say my spacecraft was down this hall!"

But at the end of the hall are two doorways. "Which door?" asks Sunstreaker.

"I don't know," Sarah admits.

Someone has to make a decision quickly. Flip a coin.

If it comes up heads, take the door to the left and turn to page 67.

If the coin comes up tails, take the door to the right and turn to page 43.

"Ms. Sanders," says Kup politely, "we need the secret of the Invisibility Device."

"Sorry." Sarah's voice is firm. "It's too dangerous."

"But—but we need it to help us defeat our enemies, the Decepticons!" cries Hot Rod. "Believe me, you wouldn't want them to rule the Earth. Your device will help us fight them."

"That's just it!" says Sarah. "I don't want my invention used for war of any kind!"

But just then the scream of jet engines fills the air!

"The Decepticons!" gasps Kup. "They must have seen the ship flickering in the air!"

And now the Decepticon jets attack!

Wham! A blast sends rock and sand flying!

Crash! A second blast rattles the spacecraft!

Bam! A third blast hits so close that Sarah is knocked right off her feet! The Invisibility Device flies from her arms and falls to the ground several yards away.

"Come on!" Hot Rod tells Sarah as she scrambles up again. "We've got to get you out of here!"

"But—but the device—"

"No time to go back for it!" Hot Rod cries, and quickly transforms into his auto mode. "Jump in and let's get going!"

The two Autobots and Sarah whiz out of firing range. Kup hastily glances back.

. . . .

Turn to page 26.

"The Decepticons aren't following us!" Kup says. "They're landing to look at the spacecraft. Come on, let's hide among these rocks and spy on them!"

"There's Galvatron," whispers Hot Rod.

"But the Autobots are getting away!" the Decepticon Thrust is telling the evil leader.

"Forget them for now," Galvatron orders. "I wish to know more about this human's spaceship. And about this strange box the woman was carrying!"

Sarah gasps. "Oh no! Look! He has the Invisibility Device!"

What should Kup and Hot Rod do now?

If you want them to attack right now, turn to page 8.

If you think they should try to steal the Invisibility Device back, turn to page 18.

If you're afraid the Decepticons are about to leave Earth in the spacecraft, you'd better have Hot Rod and Kup hurry back to the Autobot city for reinforcements and an Autobot spaceship. Turn to page 52.

"If the Decepticons could make it through those asteroids, so can we!" says Springer. "Hang on, everyone, here we go!"

Springer sends the Autobot ship diving, plunging, and rolling through the asteroid belt. It's like trying to run through a maze where the walls are always moving, because all the rocks are floating freely in space. One moment it looks like the ship is going to crash into an asteroid. The next moment it looks like Springer is going to win the day! But suddenly Jazz shouts, "Look out!"

Two huge asteroids are zooming toward the Autobot ship, one on the left, one on the right! In another moment the ship and everyone on board will be crushed to bits of metal!

"We've got to blast those asteroids apart!" cries Ultra Magnus. "But they're coming in so fast that there's only time for one try! And we've got to hit them both at the same time, or the one we miss will still crash into the ship!"

The blast buttons on the ship are numbered one to ten. Only some of the buttons will blast both asteroids at once. Which button should Springer hit?

. . . .

If you picked 1, 3, 5, 7, or 9, turn to page 30.
If you picked 2, 4, 6, or 8, turn to page 56.
If you picked 10, turn to page 53.

Quickly Kup outlines his plan to get the Invisibility Device back from the Decepticons. Hot Rod grins. "Sounds good to me!" he says.

"Ready?" asks Kup softly. "Then come on! Let's go!"

With that, Hot Rod and Kup begin racing back and forth at top speed to spots all over the canyon's rim above the Decepticons. They fire down at the Decepticons as they go, shooting from all sorts of different angles.

"Hey!" yells the startled Decepticon Thrust, ducking hastily. "Who's shooting at us?"

"I don't know!" shouts Starscream. "I don't see anyone!"

"Autobots!" yells Ravage. "It's got to be Autobots! But where are they? How many Autobots are there?"

"Dozens!" whimpers the cowardly Laserbeak. "It—it's got to be dozens of them! We're trapped!"

"Never mind that!" shouts the angry Starscream. "Fight back! Hurry!"

The confused Decepticons begin shooting back in all directions. The canyon echoes with explosions. Dust fills the air, and bits of shattered rock start raining down on the Decepticons.

Turn to page 64.

Both blasts strike the asteroids at the same time! There's a tremendous explosion, and the Autobot ship is battered by bits of flying rock.

"Damage report!" shouts Ultra Magnus.

"Just some dents and scratches," Prowl answers. "We've made it!"

"We sure did," says Springer modestly. "Look, there's open space ahead of us. But now where are the Decepticons?"

Where are they, indeed? Try to find out on page 48.

"Tell you what, Kup, Hot Rod," says Springer. "We'll take a good look around. But if we don't find anything, you two had better go back and get yourselves a good checkup!"

"This is a blast!" chuckles Jazz. "A sandblast!"

The Autobots spread out to search. At first they find nothing unusual, only sand and gravel, gravel and sand. But suddenly Hot Rod cries, "I've found something! Look at this!"

There's a smooth path in the sand, as though something heavy had been dragged away.

"Sorry, Hot Rod," mutters Jazz, "it looks like there really was a ship here."

"The Decepticons are the only ones on Earth besides ourselves who are powerful enough to drag off a spacecraft," observes Kup. "It looks like they've got it."

"But they won't keep it!" cries Hot Rod eagerly. "Come on!"

Springer, Hot Rod, Kup, Jazz, Prowl, and Sunstreaker follow the trail of flattened sand through the desert. For a time things go smoothly, almost too smoothly. But then suddenly the path ends when the Autobots come to rocky terrain.

. . . .

Turn to page 32.

"Now what?" wonders Jazz.

The Autobots spread out, trying to pick up the craft's trail again. But it's in vain. They can't find so much as a misplaced pebble.

But then Kup stops short. "Wait a minute!" he says sharply. "Everyone, take cover!"

What does Kup see? Hurry! Turn to page 14.

You've made a dangerous decision! Before you can catch him, Scavenger races right into a whole nest of Decepticons, who are all crowding around the spacecraft.

"Autobots are after me!" Scavenger gasps.

And now it's the Autobots' turn to flee!

. . . .

If you want the Autobots to run away, turn to page 41.

If you think the Autobots should stand and fight, turn to page 5.

Just in time, Sarah leaps to one side! The blast misses her, but the force of it throws her off her feet. Hot Rod races up in his car form.

"Get in!" he shouts to Sarah. "And hang on!"

As Dirge fires at them again, Hot Rod takes off at top speed. He leaps over dunes and zips around rocks, wildly zigzagging. Sometimes Dirge's blasts shower Hot Rod and Sarah with sand, but the Decepticon can't get a clear shot at them! When the other Autobots join them, Dirge gives up. With the Autobots close behind, Hot Rod and Sarah race back to Metroplex.

Once inside the city, Sarah says slowly, "You saved my life. I didn't want anyone to use my invention for anything but peace, but I don't want those Decepticons trying to take over Earth, either!" She hesitates. "All right," she reluctantly agrees. "I'll show you how to scramble the Invisibility Device."

Two days later the drone of fighter jets fills the air above Autobot City. The Autobots look up, but they don't see a thing.

"This is it," says Ultra Magnus. "Get out the Invisibility Scrambler!"

Turn to page 72.

The Autobots attack the Decepticons boldly, laser blasters firing away! But the Autobots are totally outnumbered! The dark halls echo with the horrible sounds of metal being torn apart as the Decepticons close in. And all too soon the Autobots have paid the price of rashness. They're soon reduced to a pile of spare parts!

"Now there'll be no stopping us!" gloats Galvatron.

He's right. With Sarah and the Invisibility Device in their possession, the Decepticons soon attack the entire planet. For the people of Earth, it's clear that this is . . .

THE END

Hot Rod is still racing through the desert with a pack of angry Decepticons close behind him. "I'll lead those Decepticons so far away from my friends they'll need a month to get back!" thinks Hot Rod.

It's a wild chase! The Decepticons are so busy chasing Hot Rod that they don't have a chance to transform and take to the air. Hot Rod zooms and dodges and whizzes around rocks on two wheels as the Decepticons shoot bursts of energy all around him!

"They'll never catch me!" he laughs.

But suddenly he comes to a screeching halt. There's a canyon in front of him, and it's wide and deep!

"Uh-oh!" gasps Hot Rod. "Now what do I do?"

. . . .

Do you think he should try to climb down the canyon wall? If so, turn to page 42.

Do you think he should try to leap the canyon? Turn to page 50.

Do you think he should try to trick the pursuing Decepticons? Turn to page 6.

"Try it now!" Prowl calls to Sarah, who quickly starts up the ship's engines. There's a groan, a whine . . . and the engines finally start to fire.

"Prepare for lift-off!" calls Prowl as the rickety craft rises off the ground.

"We're moving too slowly!" yells Hot Rod. "Sarah, you've got to give the ship more power!"

"I can't!" she yells back. "Look at those dials! Any more power and I'll burn out the engines!"

Just then a bright blast of energy whizzes by the ship.

"The Decepticons will have the range in a moment," says Prowl calmly. "Ms. Sanders, I suggest you risk it. Turn the throttle to full power."

"All right, here goes! We'll either fly or crash!" cries Sarah. "Hang on, everyone! Full speed ahead!"

. . . .

Do they make it? Or does their escape end in a fiery crash? Hurry! Turn to page 66 to find out!

"Try firing directly at the moon," Ultra Magnus orders the Autobots.

"Okay," says Springer. "Here goes!"

They fire several quick blasts of energy at the moon. Bright flashes streak the sky but fade away almost at once.

"Hey!" Jazz cries. "I thought I saw something metallic down there! Maybe it's—"

But before he can finish, a sharp explosion rocks the ship!

"The Decepticons!" gasps Kup. "We've made ourselves a perfect target for them!"

Again and again the Decepticon blasts strike the Autobot ship. Hurled from one side to the other, the Autobots are soon nothing but bits of space junk.

THE END

Hot Rod quickly transforms to his auto mode. "Come on!" he shouts. "Let's get out of here!"

He and the other Autobots roar over the rocky terrain. But the Decepticons are right behind them!

"This—this isn't going to work!" gasps Kup. "We're too easy a target! Hurry! Let's split up!"

The six Autobots shoot off in six different directions! The Decepticons screech to a halt, confused.

"That way!" yells Frenzy.

"No, no! This way!" yells Thrust.

"Idiots!" shouts Galvatron. "They're all getting away! After them!"

But before the Decepticons can move, Hot Rod does a U-turn and races back toward the Decepticons at full speed. His ultrahigh-beam headlights are dazzling! And for a moment, the Decepticons' sensors are blinded. By the time they can see clearly again, all the Autobots, including Hot Rod, are gone!

Once they're sure they've eluded the Decepticons, the Autobots reunite.

"But what happened to the young woman?" asks Springer.

The Autobots conduct a search. They find her wandering alone through the desert.

To hear her story, turn to page 65.

Quickly Hot Rod transforms to his robot mode and begins the dangerous climb down the side of the canyon. A sudden blast strikes the rock beside him. He stares up to see the Decepticon Starscream in his jet mode firing down at him! Frantically, Hot Rod fires back.

It's a hit! Starscream spirals down out of the sky and crashes in a fiery heap at the bottom of the canyon.

Then Hot Rod sees something that he can't believe. From deep in the canyon, a secret door opens and a rescue team of Decepticons comes out, hoses down Starscream, and pulls him back inside the secret door.

Hot Rod wastes no time in radioing his location to the other Autobots. Then he hides in a small cave and waits.

In minutes a full army of Autobots is attacking the canyon. They batter down the secret door and discover a Decepticon base hidden deep underground. It's not long before the brave Autobots have destroyed this newly built Decepticon base.

"Well done," Ultra Magnus congratulates Hot Rod. "Thanks to your quick thinking we not only retrieved Sarah's spaceship, but we've destroyed this secret enemy base."

"It was nothing," Hot Rod replies modestly—but deep inside, the young Autobot's circuits are humming with pride.

THE END

42

The door to the right leads to a storage closet full of Decepticon spare parts. Prowl notices a small pile of Decepticon emblems. "Hurry, put these on—and try to look mean," he directs the others, then scoops up Sarah to make it look like she's his prisoner. "Now let's try the door on the left."

The door on the left leads to a courtyard. And in the middle of that yard is the spacecraft, but it's guarded by Decepticon drones. The drones quickly scan the approaching Autobots for their emblems to see if they have clearance to be in the courtyard. Will Prowl's plan work? Or will the Autobots be blasted?

Hurry up and turn to page 16.

"We can't let the Decepticons keep Sarah's space-ship *or* the Invisibility Device!" says Jazz.

"Certainly not," agrees Prowl. "We must overtake them before they have time to study the device."

"Then what are we waiting for?" cries Hot Rod.

He and the other Autobots zoom off. And soon they find the Decepticons in a narrow canyon, busily going over the spacecraft.

"They'll detect us any second!" whispers Hot Rod. "We'll have to attack!"

But there are an awful lot of Decepticons down there! Do you think a direct attack is such a good idea? Maybe Prowl can come up with a better one.

. . . .

If you decide to attack, using the element of surprise, turn to page 61.

If you'd rather see if there's a chance for Prowl to come up with a better idea, turn to page 22.

Hot Rod can't control himself. He grabs the box from Sarah. "Wow! With this we could beat the Decepticons in a snap," he says excitedly.

"Hey, that's my invention! Give it back to me!" Sarah cries.

Hot Rod hesitates, but then his greedy side wins out over his sense of fairness. "Sorry, lady, we need this more than you do," he says. "You'll be glad we have it, anyway, 'cause we're going to use it to keep your planet safe from the Decepticons."

"Now, Hot Rod," Kup warns, "give the lady back her—"

It's too late. Hot Rod has already transformed into his auto mode and is zooming back to the Autobot city with his prize. "I'll be a big hero when I show our leader, Ultra Magnus, this Invisibility Device," Hot Rod thinks happily. He is busily dreaming of how the Autobots will battle the Decepticons invisibly when . . . *kar-a-barooooom!*

The Invisibility Device had a self-destruct explosion button and Hot Rod accidentally triggered it when he went over a bump. Now his dreams of glory have gone, well, all to pieces.

THE END

Ultra Magnus listens to Jazz's plan and nods. "Let's do it," he says. "Shut off all power in the ship." Quickly he explains the plan to Springer, then adds, "Now, everybody keep silent!"

The other Autobots haven't heard the plan and they aren't quite sure what's going on, but they trust Ultra Magnus. They obey. The Autobot ship floats silently through space. Since no one aboard it is using any power, it can't be picked up on any sensors. And since the sun's light is blocked by the moon and all lights are off on the ship, it can't be seen, either.

"Get ready, Springer," Ultra Magnus whispers. "Ready . . . now!"

At Ultra Magnus's signal, Springer launches a small probe. Suddenly it's very clear that the Decepticons *are* on the moon! When they see the probe's rocket, they think it's the Autobot ship and start firing. Now the Autobots know exactly where the Decepticons are hiding!

"Open fire!" shouts Ultra Magnus.

Bolts of energy split the darkness of space! Again and again the rocky lunar surface is lit up by explosions as the Autobots' shots strike home. Suddenly the Autobot ship is rocked by a lucky Decepticon shot!

· ·

Turn to page 60.

46

There's nothing all around the Autobot ship but space, endless, endless light-years of space. There's nothing to hear and nothing to see.

And then, all at once, Hot Rod tenses.

"It's funny, but I could almost swear someone's watching us!"

"That's right!" agrees Jazz. "I don't see anyone at all, but it *feels* as though we're being watched! And I don't think the watchers are friendly!"

"The Decepticons!" gasps Kup. "What if they've had a chance to figure out how to work the Invisibility Device? If they have, we're in big trouble! We'd better get out of the—"

Before he can finish, the ship is rocked by a sharp explosion!

"It's the Decepticons, all right!" shouts Springer. "They're firing at us! But where are they?"

Just then a second explosion hits them, from a different side, sending the Autobots staggering.

"They're circling around us!" cries Jazz. "And they *are* using the Invisibility Device! We can't fight what we can't see! We've got to make a run for it!"

Go on to page 49.

"Wait!" cries Kup. "Remember what Sarah told us about the device? It doesn't work perfectly yet. We may be able to use it against the Decepticons!"

The Decepticons are going to attack again at any moment. The next explosion may blast the Autobots out of space! Decide quickly!

. . . .

Should the Autobots run for it? Turn to page 51.

Or do you want them to stop long enough to hear Kup's plan? Turn to page 58.

"I've never tried anything like this, but—here goes!"

Hot Rod revs up his turbo-charged engine, backs up to give himself room—and races at full speed for the edge of the canyon!

"Yahoo!" he shouts as he soars across open space and slams down safely on the far side. "I made it!"

Behind him, the Decepticons have come to a screeching halt. *They* don't want to try that jump! Some of them are transforming to jet mode, but Hot Rod doesn't wait around to see what happens! He zooms off to safety.

"But now I've got to find out what's been happening to my friends and Sarah!" he says.

Turn to page 9 to find out.

"We're sitting ducks here!" the Autobots agree. "We've *got* to make a run for it!"

But as the Autobot ship streaks through space, the Decepticons strike! *Wham!* The Autobot ship rocks as it's hit, and the Autobots are thrown to one side.

Crash! A second blow sends them tumbling to the other side of the ship.

"The Decepticons are out there!" gasps Hot Rod. "But I can't see a thing!"

"I can't even get to the controls!" says Springer, struggling to get up.

Again and again the helpless Autobots feel their ship rocked by energy blasts. And suddenly the Decepticons fire a blast that rips the Autobot ship apart! In no time at all, the Autobots become just so many more bits of junk littering outer space.

THE END

Now that the Decepticons have the Invisibility Device, they decide to take this strange ship and fly into deep space. They need time to study the Invisibility Device and the way it works without Autobot interference. They're going into space to find that time!

Hot Rod and Kup race back to the Autobot city, Metroplex, for help. "Hurry!" Hot Rod cries to the other Autobots. "The Decepticons are going to leave Earth with an Invisibility Device! We've got to get a spacecraft ready and attack the Decepticons before they get too far away!"

"Everybody prepare for a launch!" orders the Autobot leader, Ultra Magnus.

Soon an Autobot spacecraft blasts off from Metroplex and into the blackness of space, in pursuit of the Decepticons.

"But . . . where are they?" wonders Hot Rod. "There isn't a trace of the Decepticons in all this emptiness around us!"

"What do you expect?" asks Springer, who's piloting the Autobot ship. "Space is—well, full of space! Anybody have an idea where the Decepticon ship might be?"

Find out what the Autobots think on page 59.

Bursts of energy go blazing out into space—but they miss the asteroids. The asteroids come plunging toward each other, and the Autobot ship is right between them! Springer tries desperately to get off another shot, but it's too late. Metal tears and crushes like tin foil. The asteroids crash together. And the Autobot ship and the Autobots themselves are just . . . spaced out.

THE END

Kup and Hot Rod transform into their robot modes and duck behind the tall rock. In minutes the hatch of the spacecraft is pushed open and a woman climbs out. She pulls off her hat and shakes out her long brown hair. She stares at her spacecraft in disgust. In her arms she holds a box the size of a toaster oven.

Before Kup can stop him, Hot Rod impetuously steps out from behind the rock. The startled woman shrieks at the sight of him.

Kup runs up beside Hot Rod and tries to calm the woman. "We won't hurt you," he tells her. "We Autobots are friends to Earthlings."

"I . . . ah . . . I've heard of you," the young woman says, "but I always thought it was just a crazy story kids liked to tell."

"We're real enough, you can bet on that!" boasts Hot Rod.

"So I see," the woman murmurs, still not believing her eyes. Something in Hot Rod's friendly, boyish manner reassures her, though.

"I'm Sarah Sanders," she tells the Autobots after a moment. "I'm a scientist and I've been working on a project with money I got from a research grant."

"Is that one of your inventions there?" asks Hot Rod, pointing to the box she carries.

. . . .

Turn to page 19.

A well-aimed laser burst blasts the left-hand asteroid into space dust. But the right-hand burst is too late! The Autobots are hurled about like toys as the asteroid crashes with full force into their ship!

"Full reverse power!" Ultra Magnus shouts to Springer.

The engines whine and groan but nothing happens.

"Full reverse power!" Ultra Magnus repeats. "Springer, get us out of here!"

"I don't think the engines can take it!" Springer cries.

"They've got to take it!" says Ultra Magnus. "If another asteroid hits us, we've had it!"

"All right," says Springer. "As the Earthlings would say, cross your fingers!"

Slowly the damaged ship creeps back out of the asteroid belt. The controls don't always answer Springer's signals, and the Autobots freeze as asteroids graze the ship again and again. Then, suddenly, the Autobot ship is free, back in open space!

"Damage reports!" orders Ultra Magnus. When he hears the results of those reports, he shakes his head.

"We can't go after the Decepticons like this," he says sadly. "We'll have to go back to Earth for a new ship."

Do the Autobots make it?

. . . .

Turn to page 11 to find out.

Kup quickly explains his plan to Ultra Magnus. The Autobot leader nods. It's worth a try!

"Listen to me, all of you! Be ready to fire. But fire *only at my command*! No one is to fire before that, no matter what happens!"

The Autobots agree. And then the Decepticons attack again! The Autobots tense, but they obey Ultra Magnus and hold their return fire. They wait . . . and wait . . . as the ship is rocked by blast after blast from their invisible enemy. Surely the Autobot ship can't hold together much longer!

And then it happens! Just as Sarah had said, the Invisibility Device isn't working properly. Just for an instant it fails, and the Decepticon ship is suddenly visible.

"Now!" shouts Ultra Magnus. The Autobots open fire—and blow the Decepticon ship into space dust!

"The Invisibility Device must have been lost in the explosion," says Hot Rod after a moment.

Ultra Magnus nods. "Yes. But it has done its job well. It has made the Decepticons invisible—once and for all!"

THE END

"The Decepticons could be anywhere!" says Hot Rod, looking out at space.

"No, they couldn't," corrects Kup. "They weren't that far ahead of us. Hmm! They might be hiding on Earth's moon."

"They could be heading into the asteroid belt beyond Mars," suggests Prowl. "That would be a good place to hide."

"Or," adds Springer darkly, "they could already have figured out how to use the Invisibility Device."

Where *is* the Decepticon ship?

. . . .

If you think the Decepticons are hiding on the dark side of the moon, turn to page 10.

If you think they're heading into the asteroid belt beyond Mars, turn to page 17.

If you think that the Decepticons have figured out how to use the Invisibility Device and are now lying in wait for the Autobots, turn to page 48.

59

The Autobot ship is damaged but still functioning. Quickly the Autobots start up the engines.

"The Decepticons are trying to get off the moon!" cries Hot Rod.

"They won't make it!" says Springer, aiming carefully.

He fires—and scores a direct hit on the Decepticon ship! There's a blinding explosion! It's so bright that the whole dark side of the moon is suddenly no longer dark. But just as quickly, the light fades away into darkness once more. . . .

"It's over," says Kup softly. "Too bad the Invisibility Device blew up with the Decepticon ship."

Ultra Magnus straightens proudly. "The Invisibility Device may have been destroyed," he says, "but so is the Decepticon menace—at least for now!"

THE END

The Autobots roar down the canyon at full speed! Their tires screech! Their engines scream! Their horns blare as every Autobot headlight is turned on at full blazing power!

The Decepticons are too startled to move. In the darkness they find the sudden high-intensity light blinding. In the few seconds that the Decepticons are stunned by the light, Hot Rod has just enough time to transform into his robot mode, snatch up the Invisibility Device, and transform again into his auto mode.

The Decepticons quickly mobilize, but they are too late. The Autobots have already encircled them and are firing all the weaponry at their command. The Decepticons are trapped inside this circle of light and firepower.

Hot Rod breaks out of the circle and drives away from the fight. When the other Autobots see that he has escaped safely with the device, they peel out after him, leaving the immobilized Decepticons behind.

"Haha!" laughs Hot Rod. "Even without the Invisibility Device we blinded them with our brilliance."

"Yes," agrees Kup. "When I tell of this battle in the future, I think I'll call it the Decepticon Dazzle!"

THE END

"Aha!" says Prowl to himself as a sudden idea strikes him. "Of course!" And he quickly whispers his idea to the other Autobots. They watch anxiously as the Decepticons move closer to Sarah. . . .

"Now!" shouts Prowl.

Jazz begins to create a dazzling sound and light show using his full-spectrum beacon and 180-decibel stereo speakers. Colors flash through the whole hall, blinding, quickly changing colors that go from red to green to yellow and back again. Shapes appear and disappear, first looking like Autobots, then looking like strange creatures from outer space! Now there's the roar of spaceship engines, now there's a pounding disco beat in the air, and the Decepticons whirl around and around, trying to figure out what's happening! They don't know what's hitting them! They can't tell light from shadow, left from right, even up from down!

"We're under attack!" yells Galvatron at last.

As the bewildered Decepticons scramble for their battle stations, Sarah runs out of the room and smack into the Autobots. She screams.

"Shhh!" says Kup. "We're Autobots. Friends. Follow us."

"I—I don't have much choice!" gasps Sarah.

Turn to page 24.

"No!" yells Ravage. "Don't shoot to the left! They're hiding up there on the right!"

"No, they aren't!" shouts Thrust. "Shoot to the left!"

"To the right, I tell you!" screeches Ravage.

While the Decepticons are arguing and shooting and trying to figure out where the attack is actually coming from, Hot Rod steals quietly down from the canyon rim. No one spots him. The young Autobot looks around quickly. Aha! The Decepticon Shockwave is clutching the Invisibility Device in his robot arms! Hot Rod carefully steals up behind him.

"Hey, wait a minute!" Hot Rod says to himself. "There's the Decepticon leader, Galvatron! He's nearer to me than Shockwave—and his back is turned! Maybe I should forget about the Invisibility Device for the moment and try to wipe out Galvatron!"

What do you think?

. . . .

If you want Hot Rod to risk attacking Galvatron, turn to page 13.

If you think he should just concentrate on retrieving the Invisibility Device from Shockwave, turn to page 71.

64

The young woman stares at the Autobots. "You're not . . . with the other robots, are you?"

"The Decepticons? No way!" says Hot Rod fiercely.

"We're your friends," Kup assures the woman, and quickly introduces himself and the other Autobots.

"I'm Sarah Sanders," the young woman says.

"But why were the Decepticons after you?" asks Springer.

Sarah hesitates. "You . . . did save me," she says hesitantly. "All right, I guess I can trust you. I'm a scientist, working on a college grant, and I managed to develop a spacecraft with an Invisibility Device built into the control panel. But lately I've been followed. I don't know by whom, but—but I'm scared. They might be foreign spies!" The young woman shivers. "My invention is too dangerous. I was going to destroy it and all my notes by crash-landing the spacecraft into the ocean and bailing out at the last minute. But the craft broke down here in the desert."

"And now the Decepticons have both the spacecraft and the Invisibility Device," says Prowl grimly.

What should the Autobots do now?

. . . .

Should they get Sarah to build them an Invisibility Device so they can fight back when the Decepticons attack them? Turn to page 3.

Should they continue to search for Sarah's craft? Turn to page 44.

Blast after blast of energy blazes around Sarah's struggling spacecraft. Slowly the craft picks up speed. There's the burning smell of overheated machinery as the engines begin to whine.

"Are the Decepticons going to shoot us down," wonders Sarah nervously, "or are we just going to crash?"

But now the Invisibility Device flickers on again, and the rest of the Decepticon shots go wide! The Autobots and Sarah cheer as the spacecraft finally reaches full power and zooms away! Nothing stops their flight now, and soon they're safe in the Autobot city of Metroplex.

"After seeing close up how evil the Decepticons are," says Sarah, "I want to help the Autobots in any way I can! I'll give you the plans to my Invisibility Device!"

"We'll be able to make those Decepticons disappear for good now!" laughs Hot Rod.

He's right. For the evil Decepticons, this is truly the beginning of . . .

THE END

The door to the left opens onto a courtyard. In the middle of the yard stands Sarah's spacecraft. There's only one problem: It's guarded by Decepticon droids.

The droids are scanning all who enter the courtyard for clearance. When they don't pick up the correct Decepticon emblem on the Autobots, they begin firing their laser guns immediately. At such close range, they quickly wipe out the Autobots.

Sarah is recaptured. She becomes Bombshell's slave. The Decepticons learn all about the Invisibility Device, and Earth soon becomes a big Decepticon playground.

THE END

Still teasing Hot Rod and Kup, the Autobots return home. Ratchet's examination of Hot Rod and Kup reveals only a few bits of sand and gravel.

The spacecraft is forgotten—for a few days. Then it happens! A swarm of crafts identical to the one spotted by Hot Rod and Kup descend without warning on Metroplex! Everyone is caught off guard! And those spacecraft are equipped with neuron beams which crumble the Autobot city and the Autobots in seconds!

The Decepticon leader, Galvatron, arrives to survey the damage.

"Wonderful!" he gloats. "If they had found our test craft that night when it broke down, they could have taken this weapon for themselves! Luckily the Autobots never returned and we had the time to retrieve the craft, perfect it, and build a whole fleet! Now we've won! Both Earth and Cybertron will be ours!"

THE END

"Not so fast," warns Kup. "Maybe this is a Decepticon trick. That thing could be crawling with Decepticons. They'd just love to get their grimy hands on one of their Autobot enemies."

"Well, do you think we should go back for some other Autobots to back us up?" asks Hot Rod.

The Autobots can't decide. The choice is yours.

. . . .

If you think Kup and Hot Rod should investigate the spacecraft right away, turn to page 54.

If you smell a Decepticon trap, have Hot Rod and Kup go to the Autobot city of Metroplex for a backup team on page 20.

69

With that, the frightened Sarah runs off into the desert. But high overhead, a strange jet zooms by. Galvatron, the Decepticon leader, has decided that he alone will own the secret of the Invisibility Device. And he's sent out the Decepticon Dirge to find the device's inventor—and destroy her!

"Death to the human!" growls Dirge, and drops a missile.

But Hot Rod has heard the sound of Dirge's engine. "Sarah! Look out!" he shouts.

. . . .

Was his warning in time? Hold your breath and turn to page 34.

Hot Rod decides to let Galvatron go and concentrate instead on retrieving the Invisibility Device. Shockwave is busy watching the other Decepticons fighting what they think is a full-scale Autobot attack. Hot Rod grins to himself.

"Here goes," he thinks, and charges Shockwave. He grabs the device from Shockwave and races off at top speed.

"Help!" Shockwave shouts to the other Decepticons. "The Autobot went that way."

The furious Decepticons race after Hot Rod. Kup sees what is happening from his hiding place on the ridge. He fires a powerful laser blast just behind the escaping Hot Rod.

The blast shatters the canyon wall, which slides down on top of the Decepticons. The Decepticons are buried in a pile of rock and rubble.

"We did it!" cries Hot Rod, rejoining Kup at the top of the canyon. "Now that Sarah sees how evil the Decepticons are, she's sure to let us use her device to fight them."

"I don't think we'll have to worry about fighting Decepticons right away," laughs Kup, looking down at the Decepticons buried in the landslide. "I think they're under too much pressure at the moment!"

THE END

The Autobots quickly set up the device Sarah built for them. It's an odd-looking little machine, full of gleaming coils and rods, and it hums loudly when Prowl switches it on. But as he points it up at the sky, the air seems to shimmer. Instantly a squad of Decepticon jets appears overhead! They don't realize they're no longer invisible!

"Fire when ready!" orders Ultra Magnus.

Blast after blast strikes the Decepticons! Taken by surprise, they haven't got time to defend themselves. Soon, every last Decepticon has been shot down by the Autobots.

As the Decepticon prisoners are taken to their cells, Starscream asks, "How did you know we were there?"

"Your plan was pretty clear," says Hot Rod. "In fact, you could say we could see right through it!"

THE END